I Like P

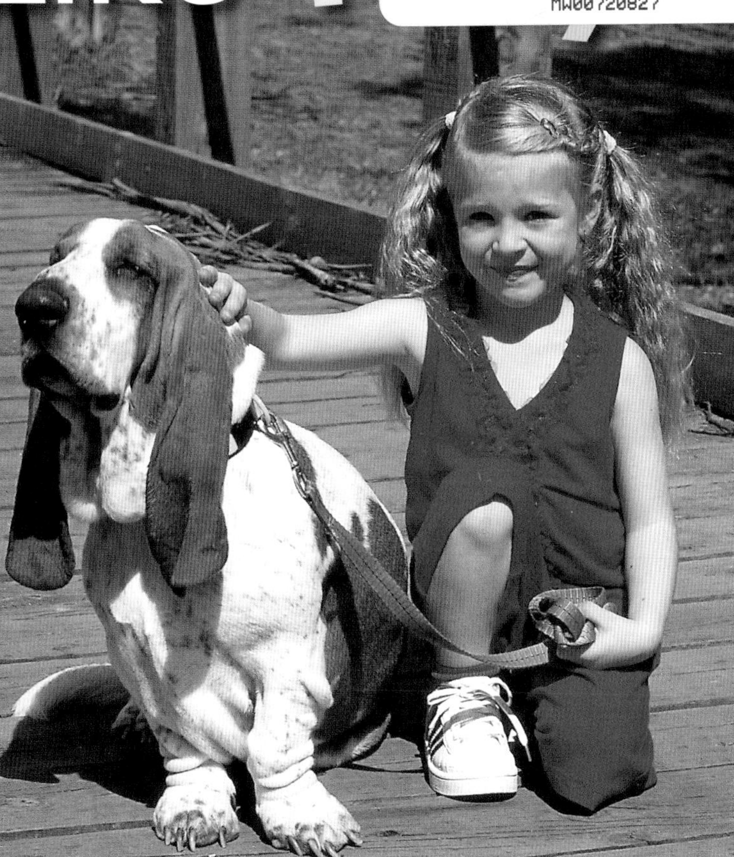

I like walking.

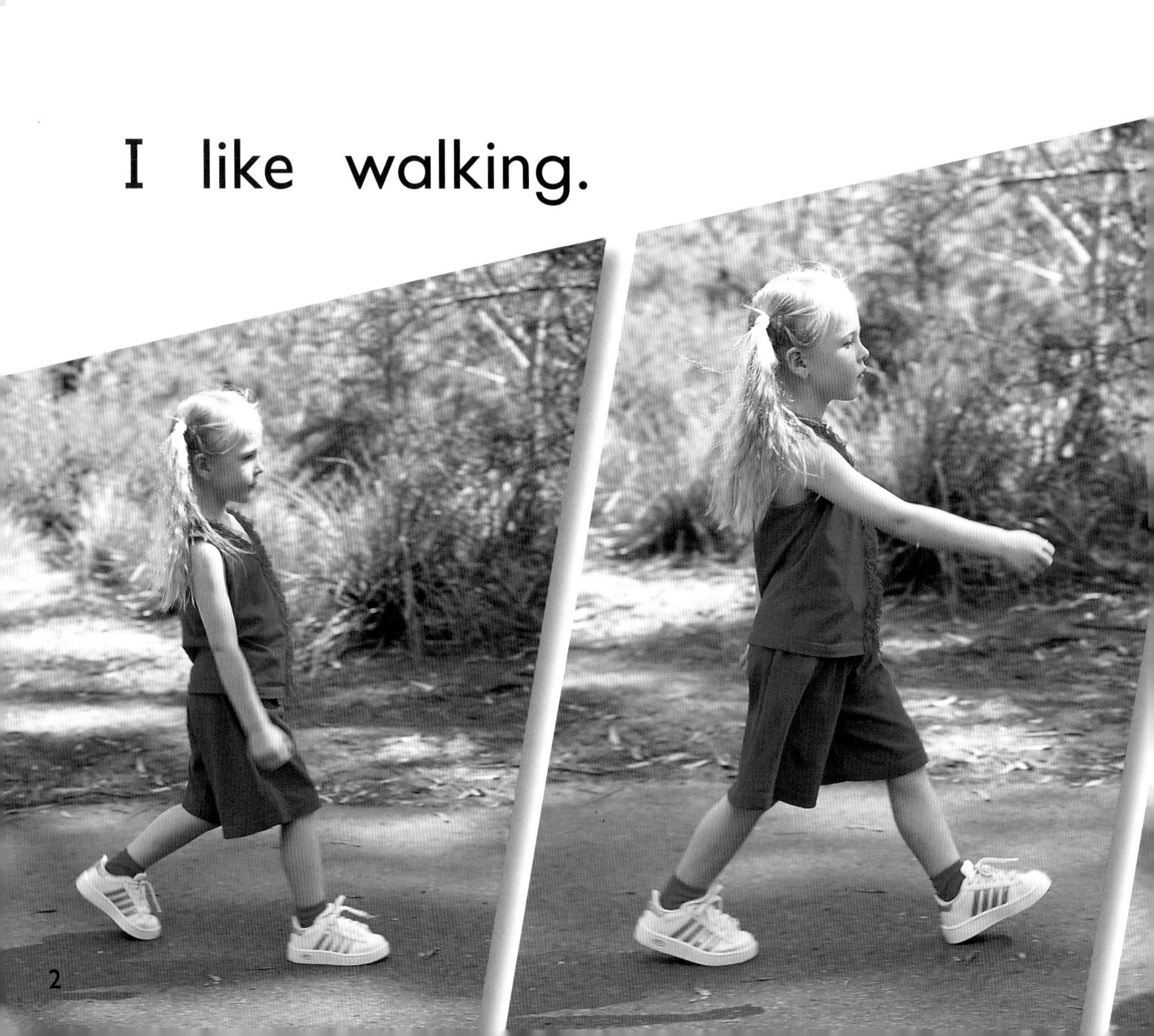

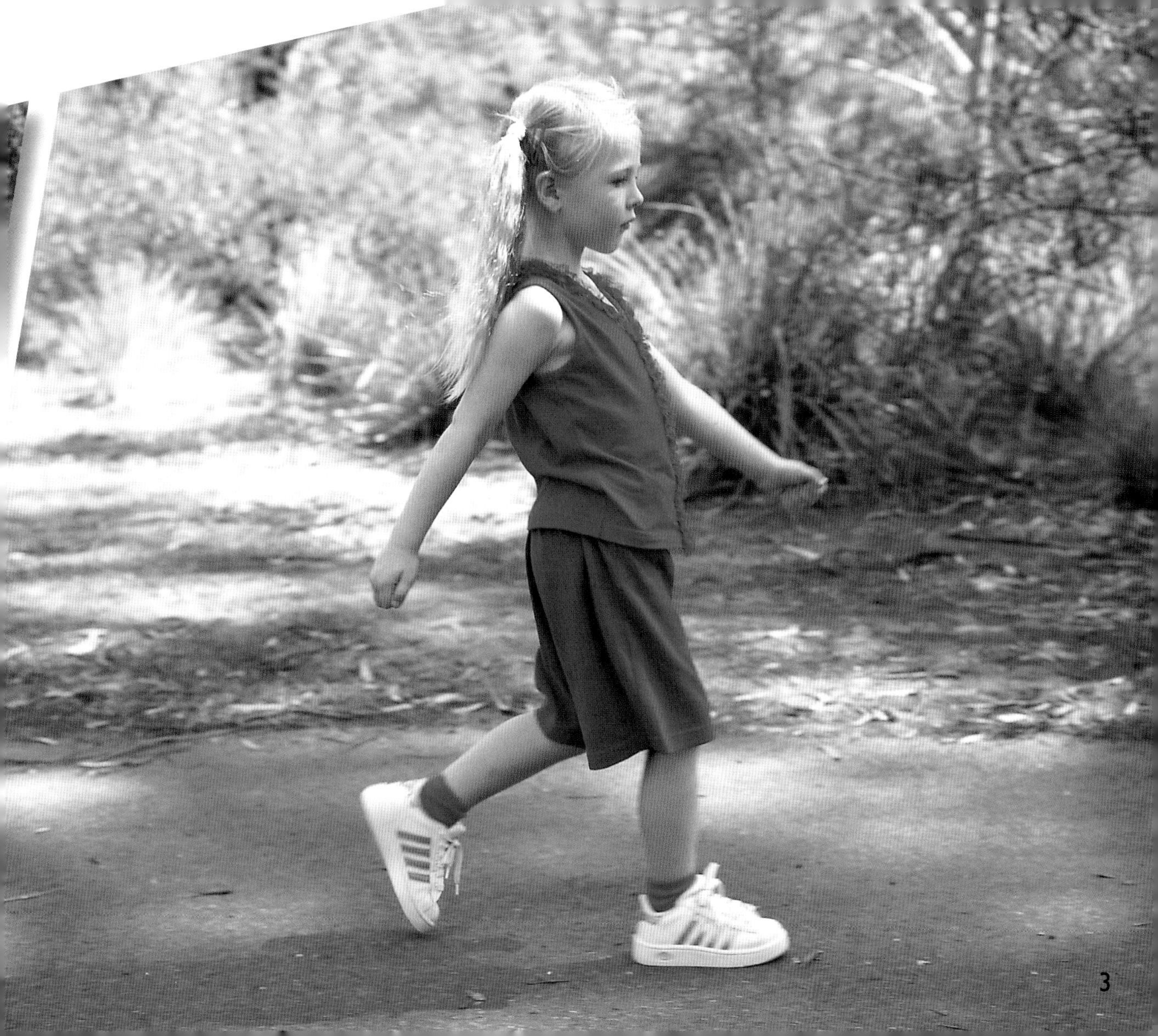

I like walking with my dog.

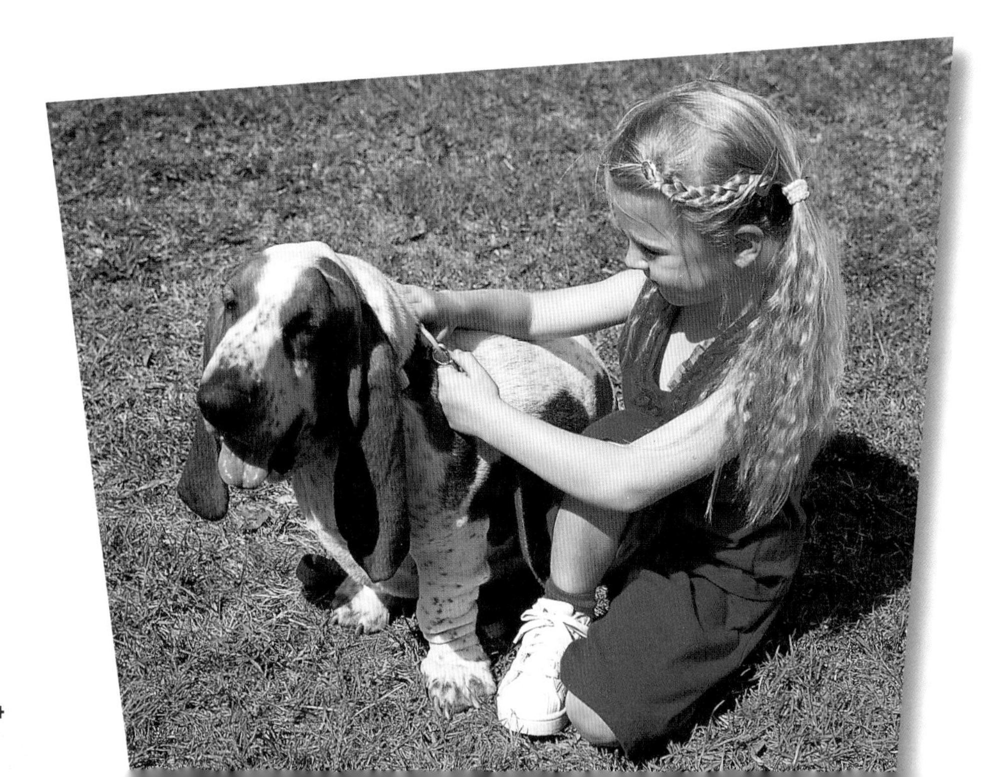

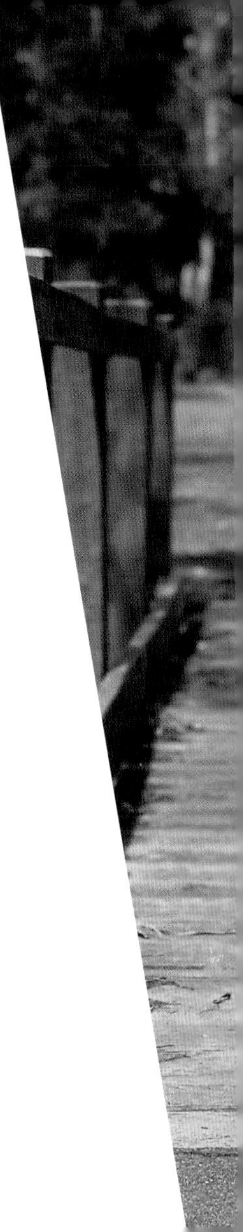

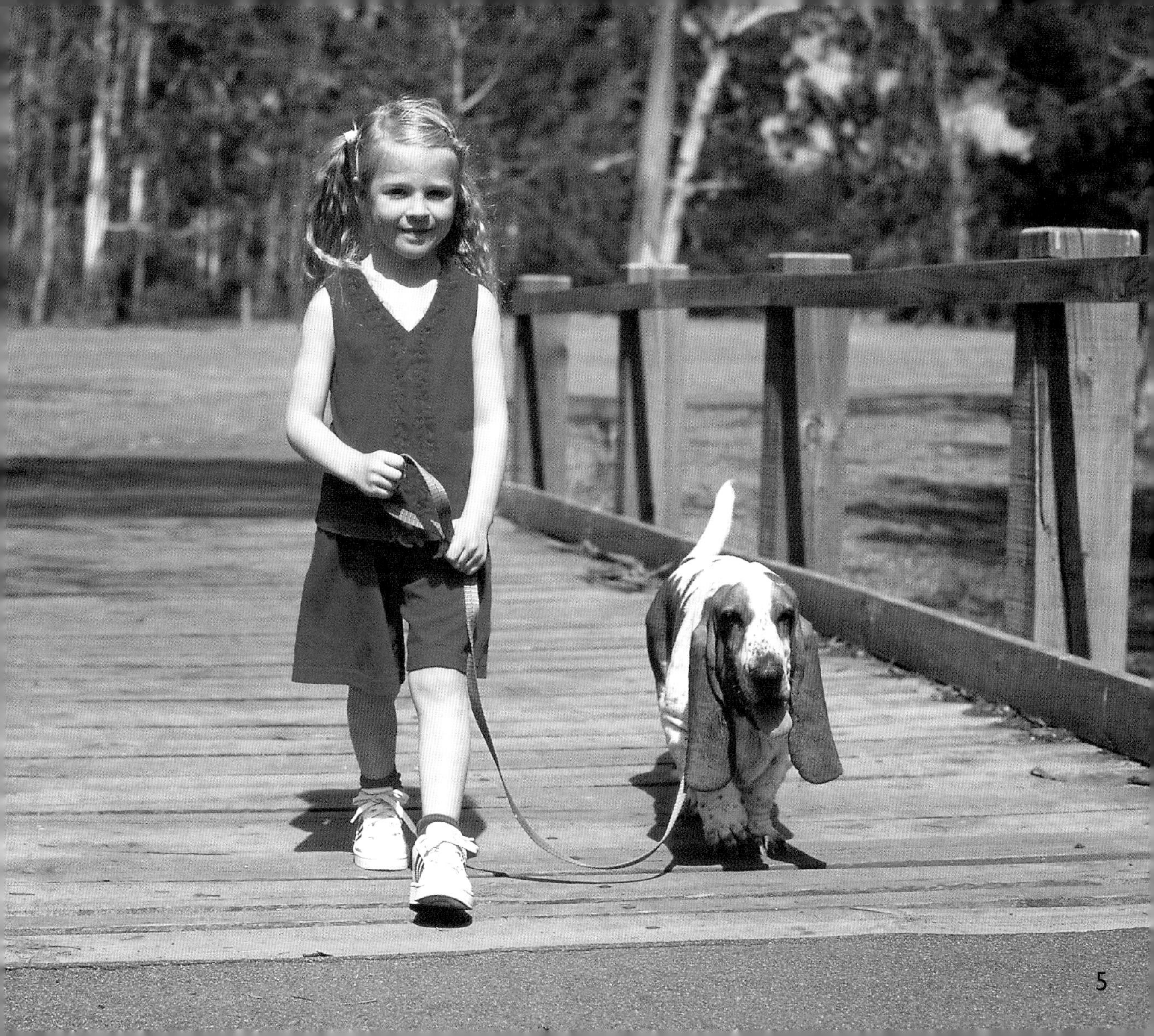

I like running.

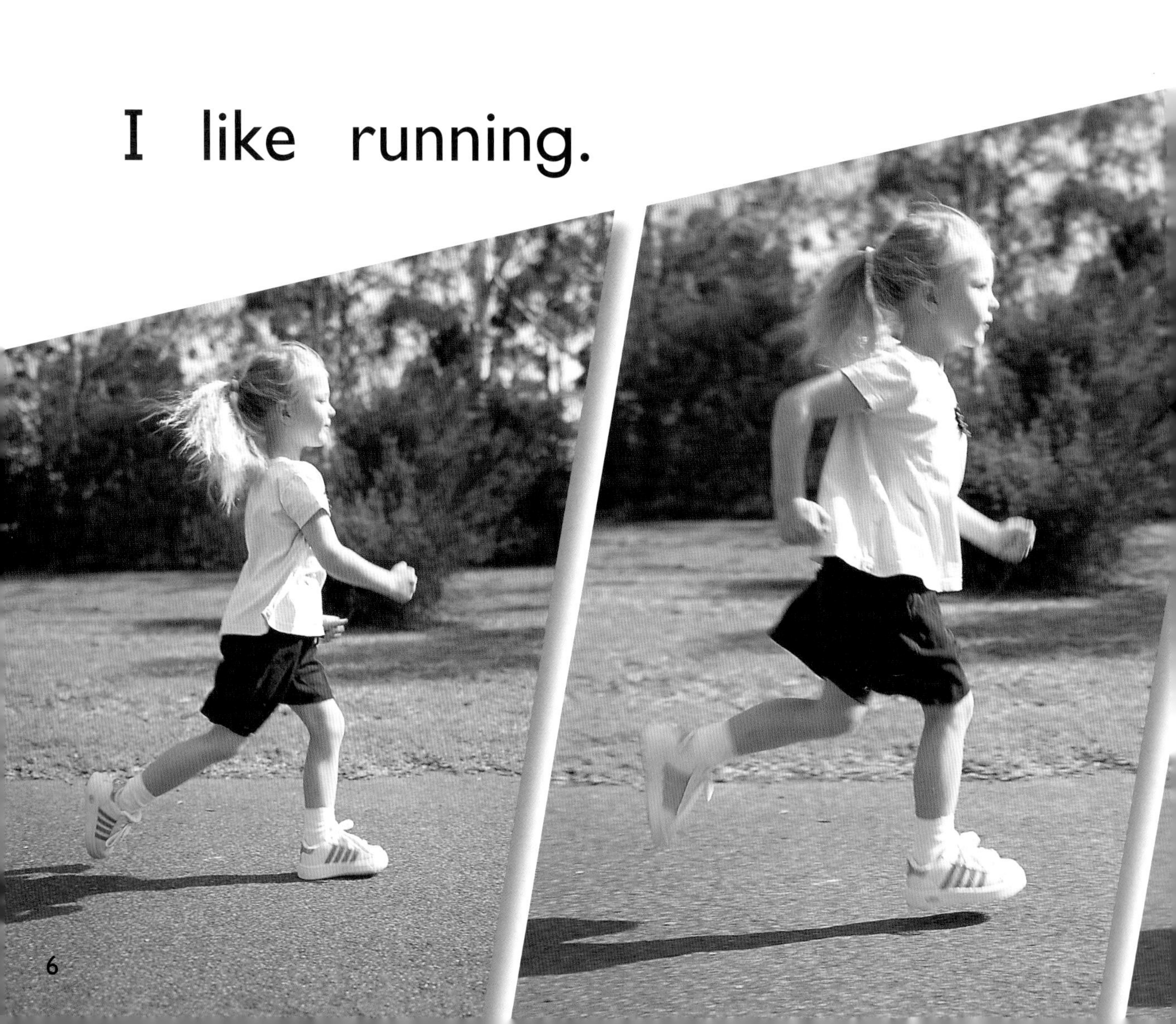

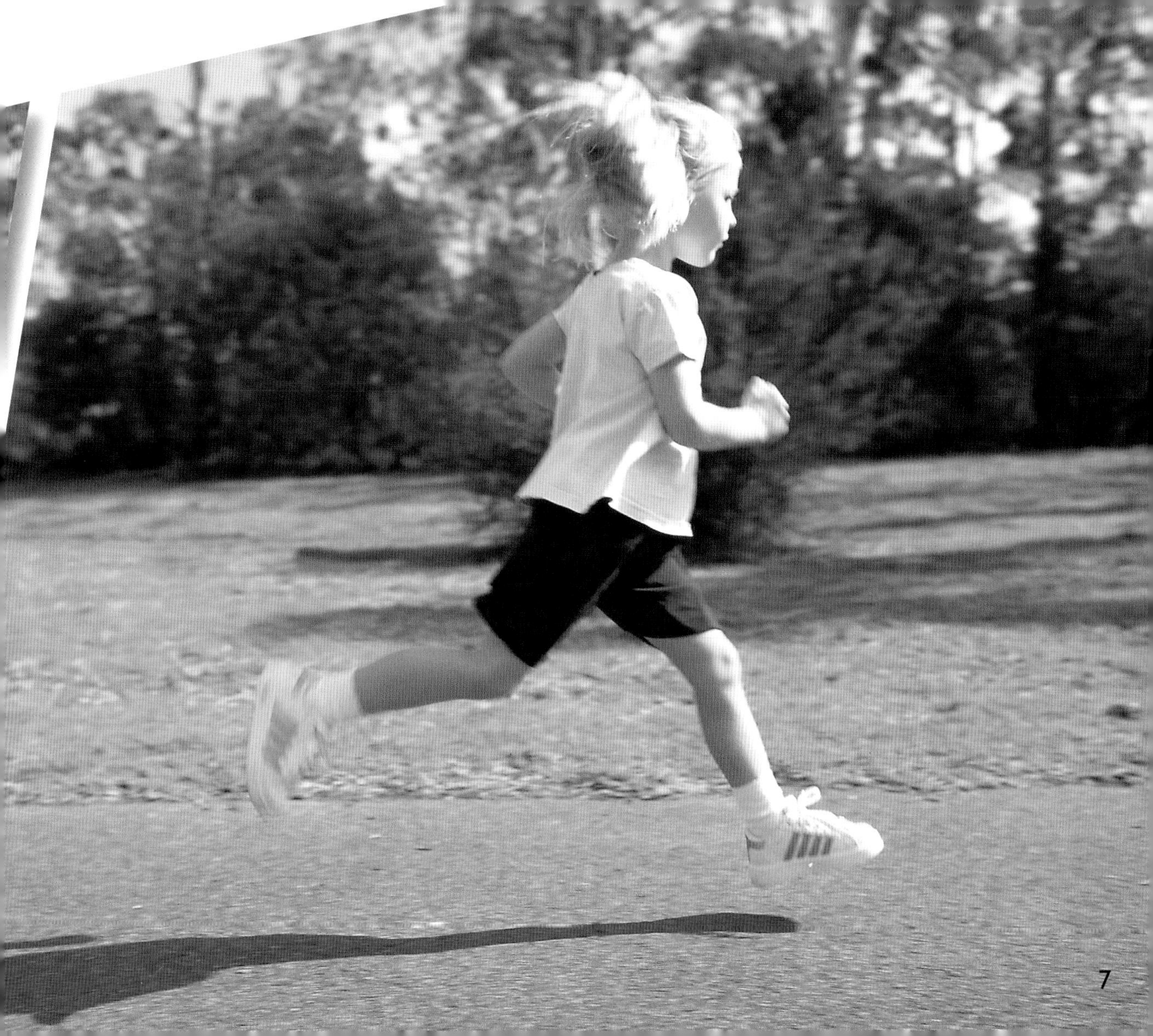

I like running

with my dad.

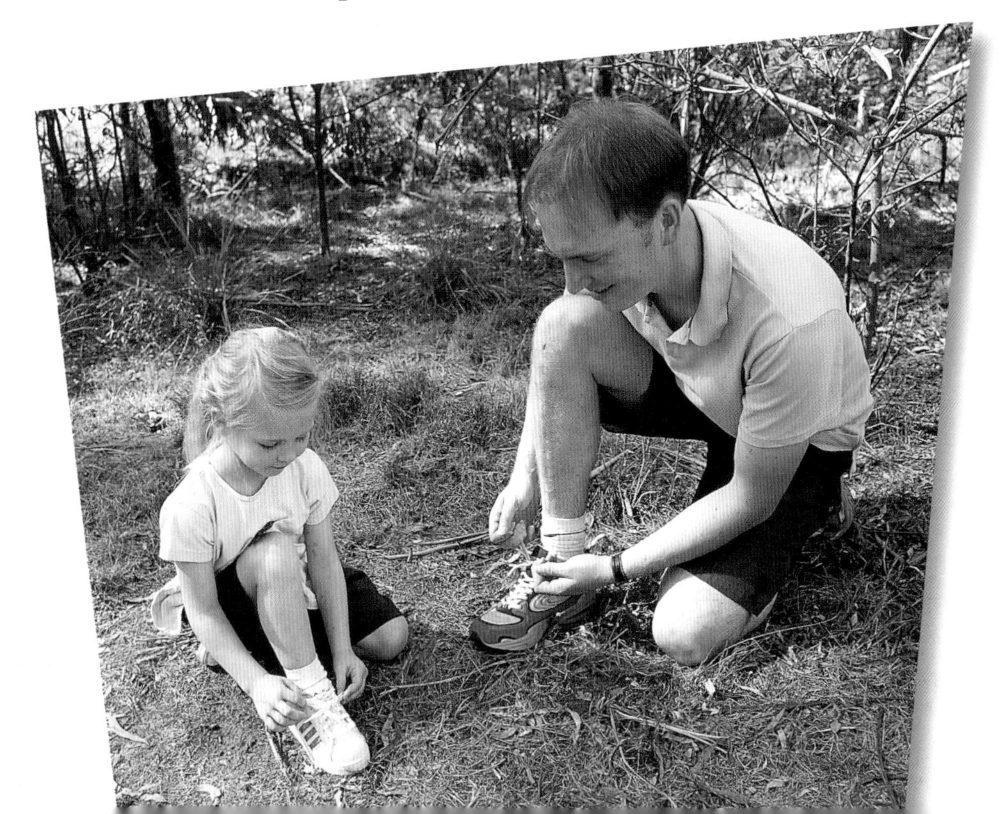

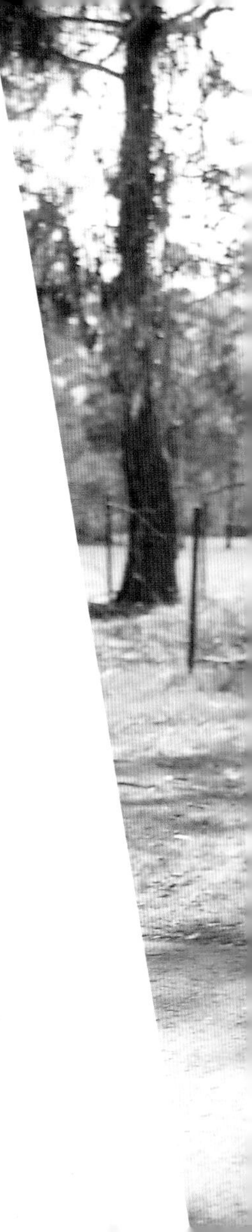

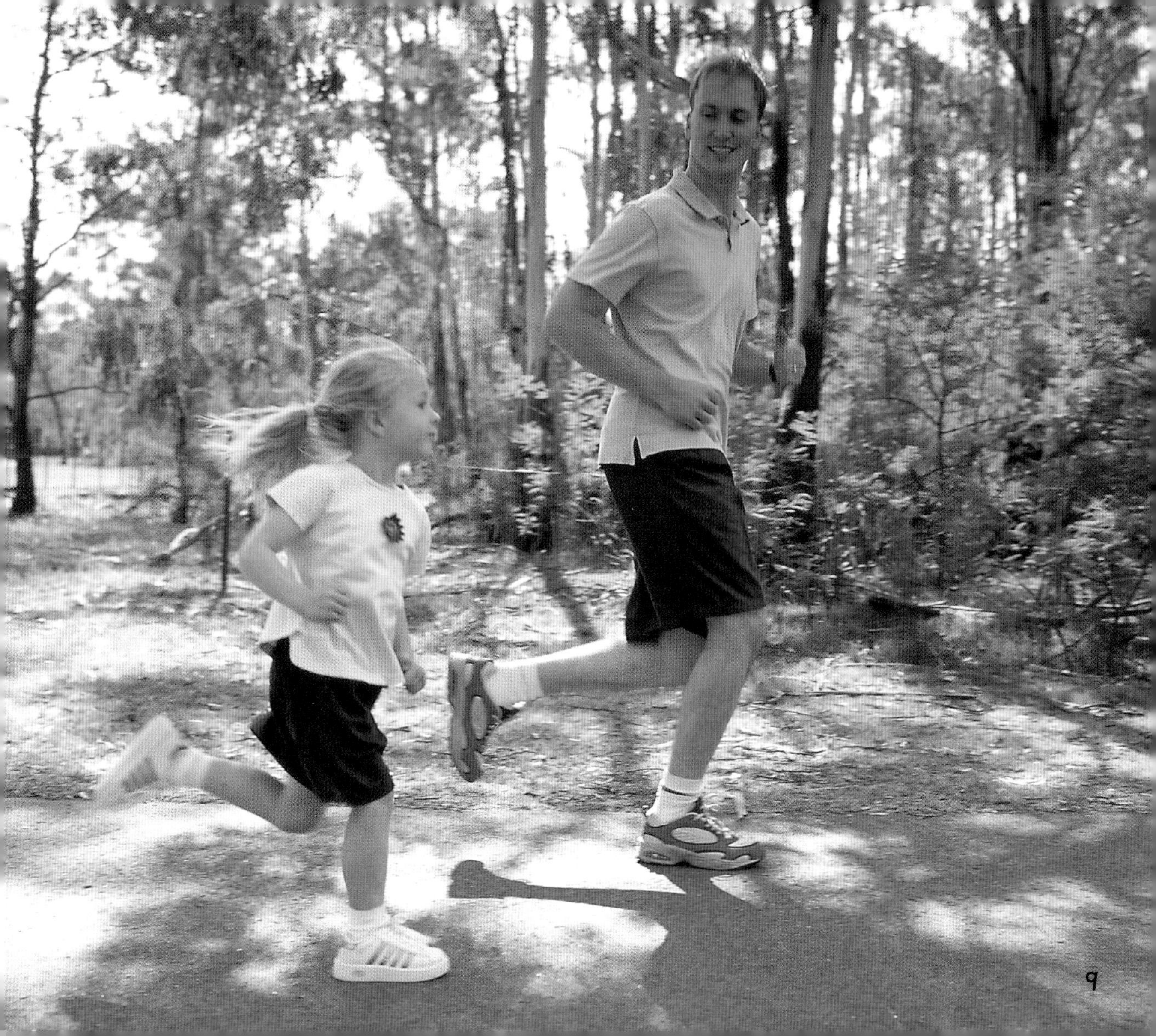

I like jumping rope.

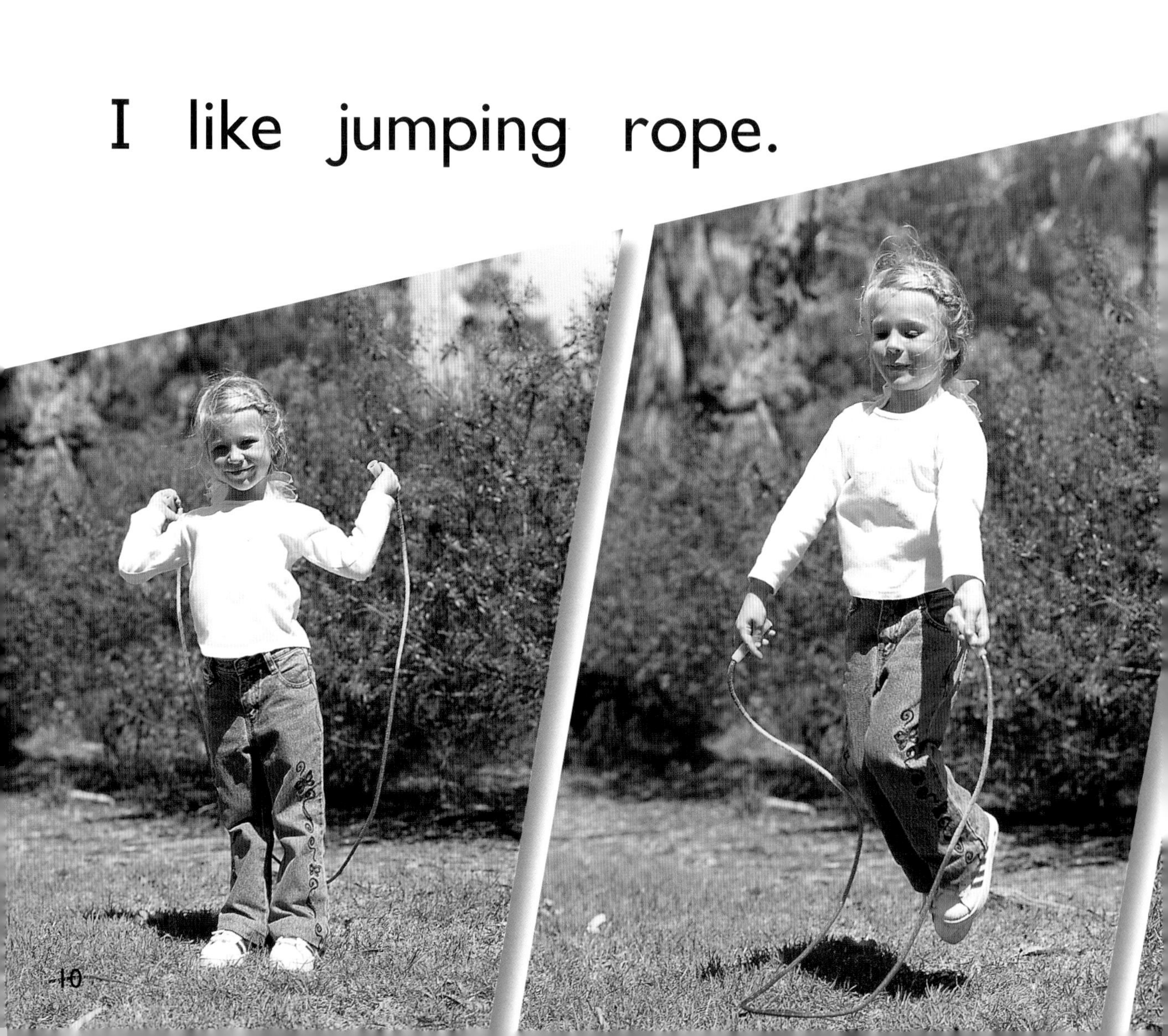

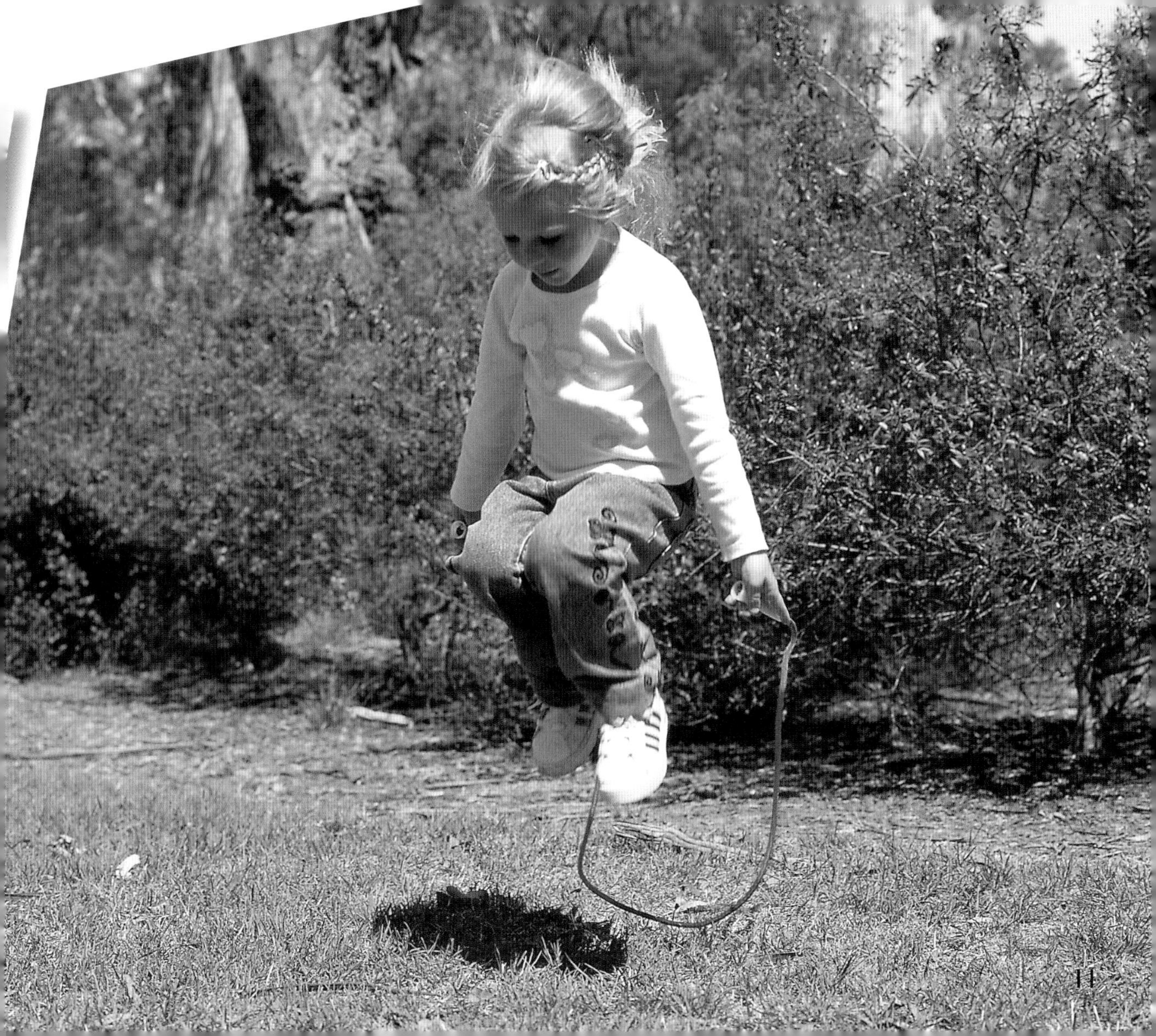

I like jumping rope with my sister.

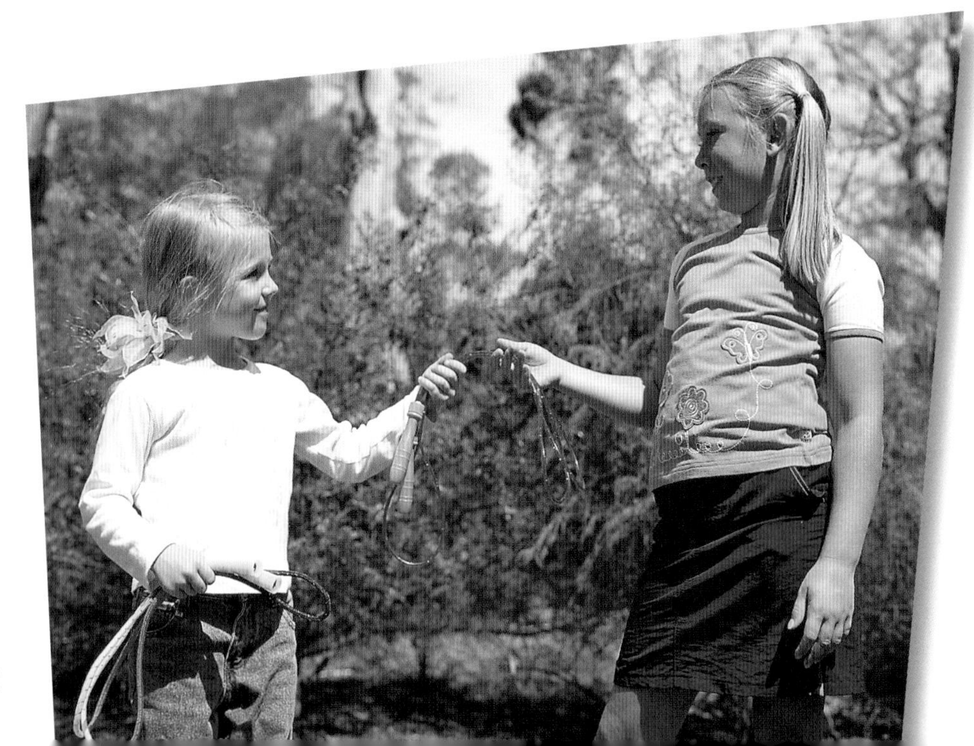

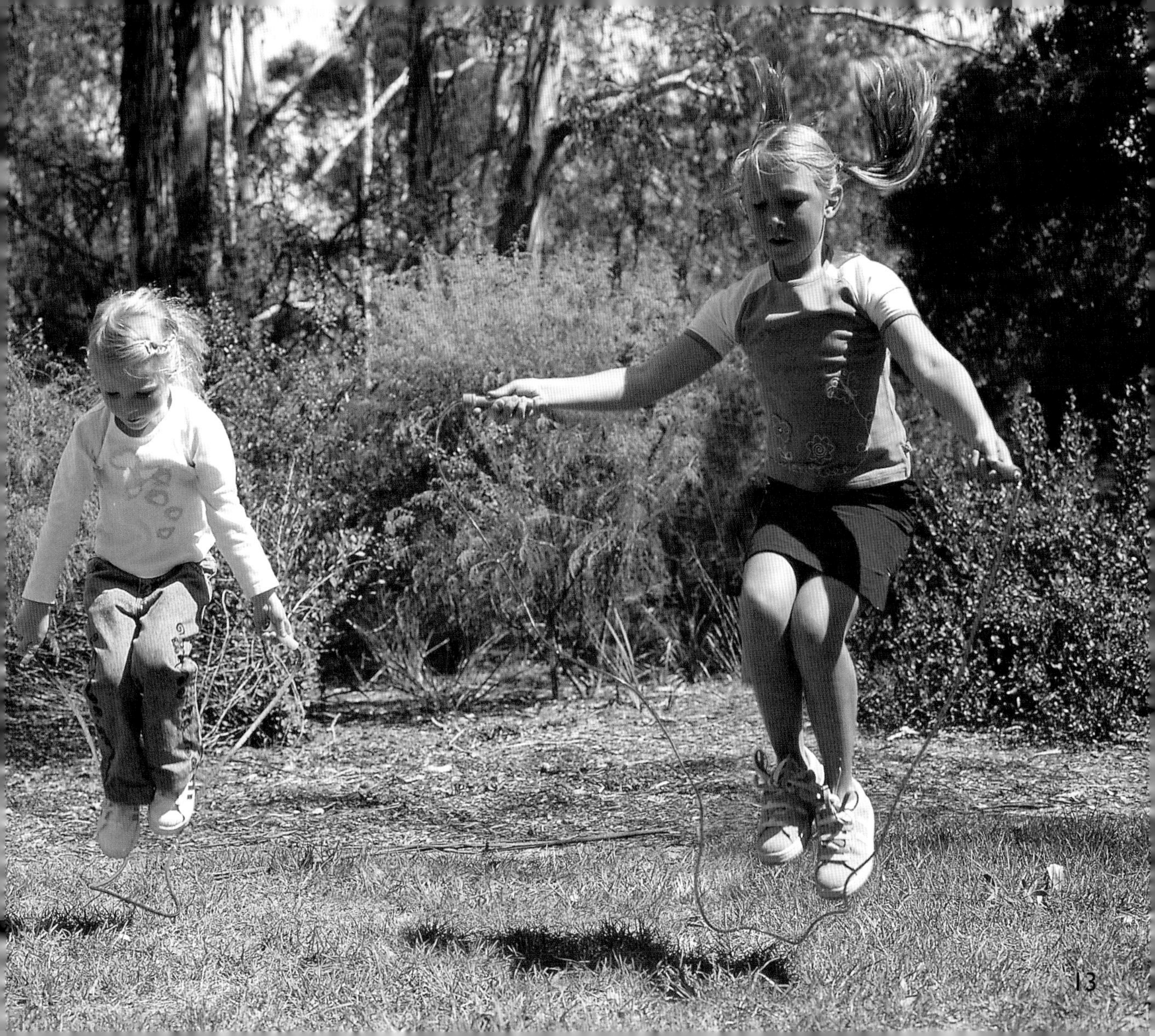

I like playing.

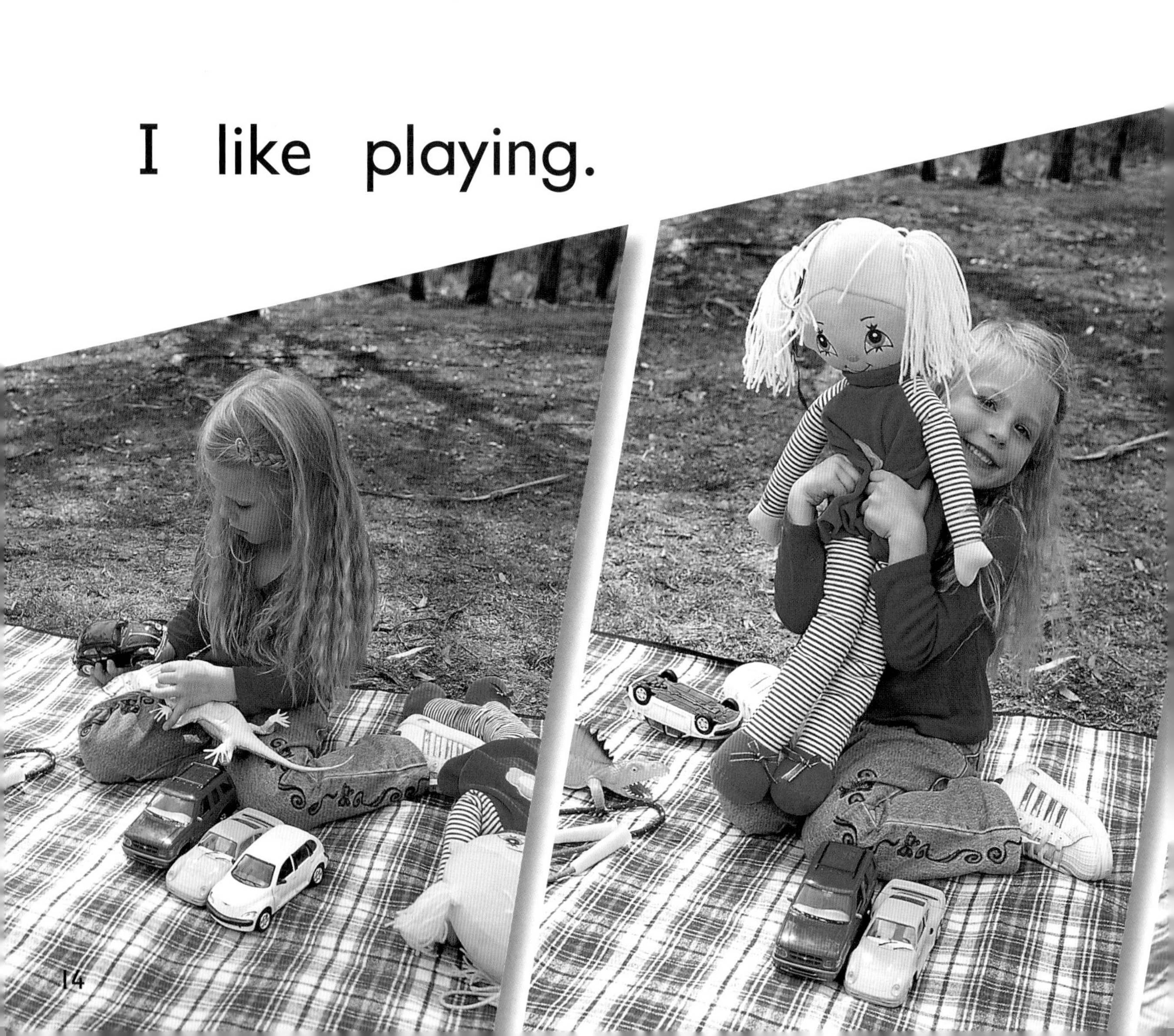

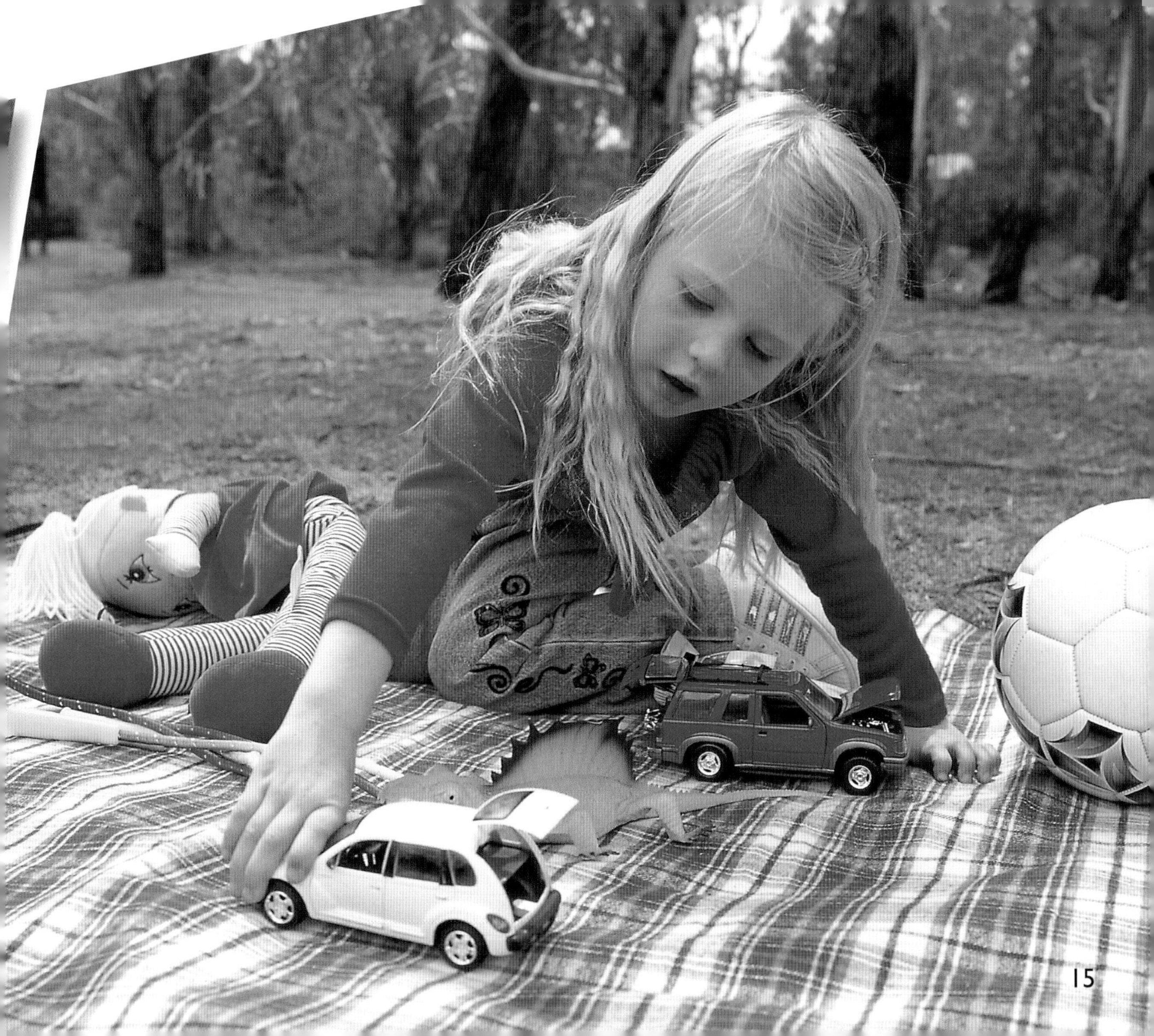

I like playing

with my friends.

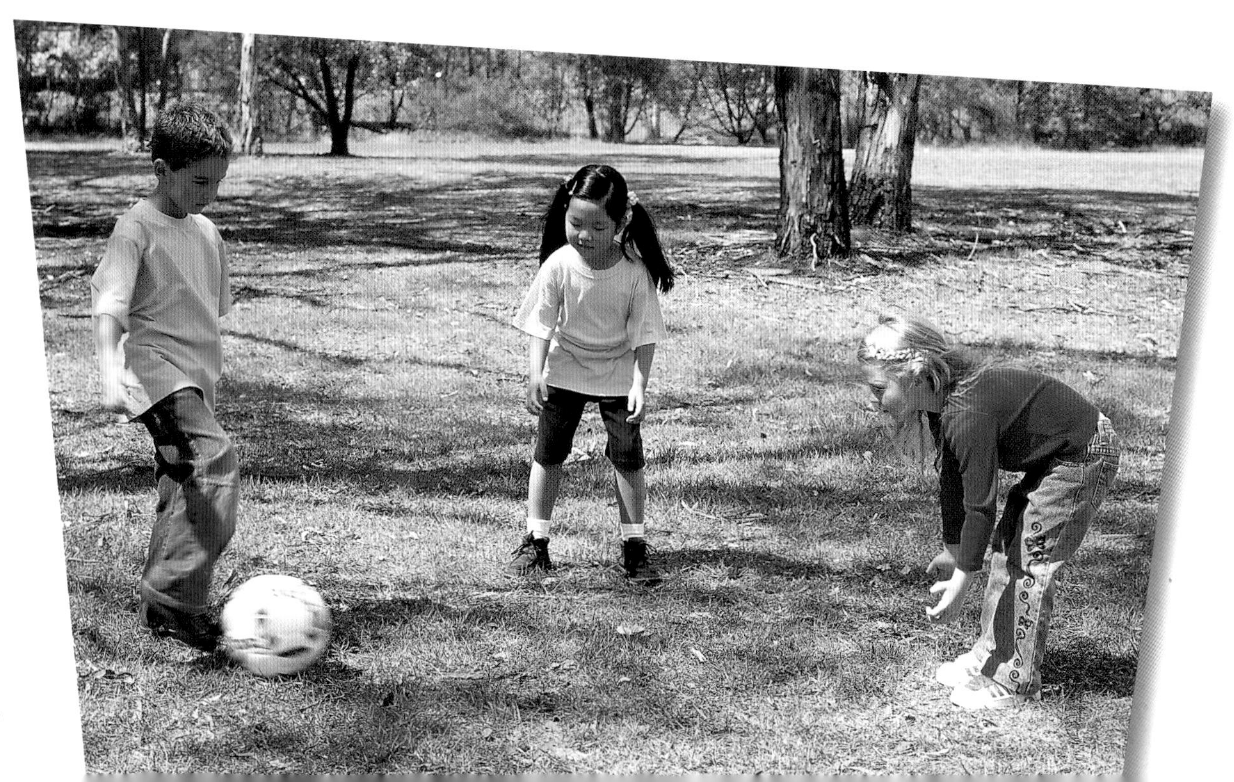